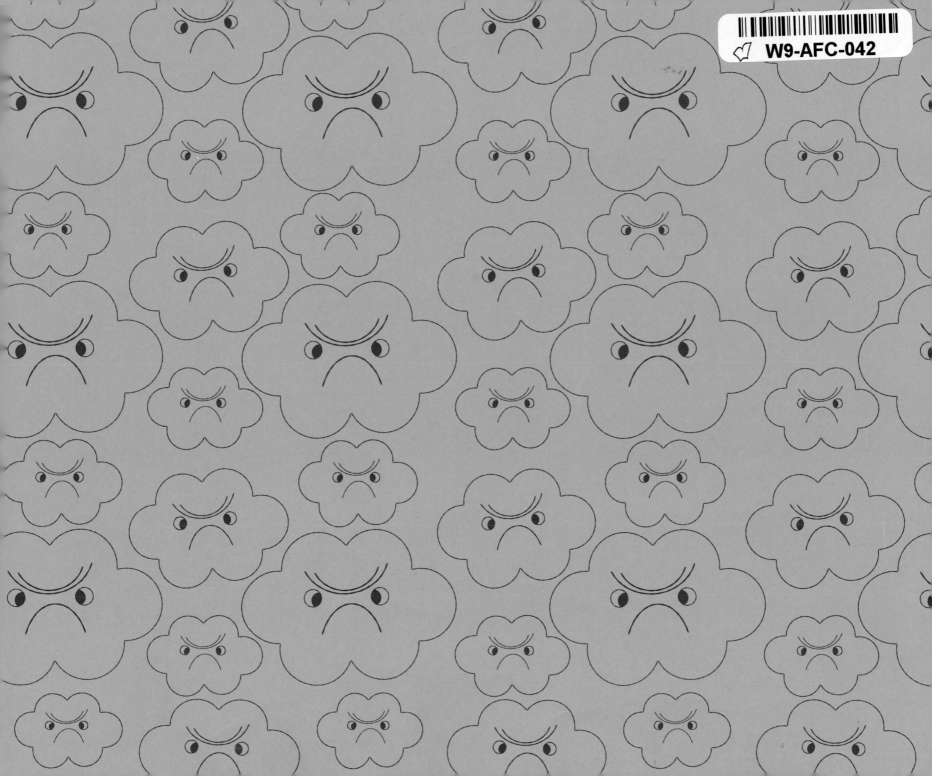

The Grouchies

To Dad and Mom, who taught me how to rhyme— DW

For Alex and Ava, who always take my grouchies away— SM

Published by
MAGINATION PRESS
An Educational Publishing Foundation Book
American Psychological Association
750 First Street, NE
Washington, DC 20002

For more information about our books, including a complete catalog, please write to us, call 1-800-374-2721, or visit our website at www.maginationpress.com.

Printed by Worzalla, Stevens Point, Wisconsin

Library of Congress Cataloging-in-Publication Data
Wagenbach, Debbie.

 The grouchies / by Debbie Wagenbach ; illustrated by Steve Mack.

      p. cm.
"American Psychological Association."
Summary: A grouchy boy learns how to chase away his grumpy moods. Includes a note to parents.
ISBN-13: 978-1-4338-0543-1 (hardcover : alk. paper)
ISBN-10: 1-4338-0543-X (hardcover : alk. paper)
ISBN-13: 978-1-4338-0553-0 (pbk. : alk. paper)
ISBN-10: 1-4338-0553-7 (pbk. : alk. paper) [1. Stories in rhyme. 2. Mood (Psychology)--Fiction. 3. Emotions--Fiction.] I. Mack, Steve (Steve Page), ill. II. Title.
PZ8.3.W1325Gr 2009

[E]--dc22

                              2009008608
10 9 8 7 6 5 4 3 2

First Printing September 2009

The Grouchies

by Debbie Wagenbach
illustrated by Steve Mack

Magination Press • Washington, DC
American Psychological Association

Today the grouchies got me. They
pushed me out of bed. They chased me down the
hallway, and this is what they said.

"Grouch and grump at everyone you meet
throughout the day. Don't be nice to anyone
and you will get your way!"

The grouchies
hovered over me
like dark clouds shade the sun.
Creeping gloomy, grumpy
thoughts took over thoughts of fun.

Then, I saw the oatmeal. I scowled and turned away. Well, I did not want oatmeal. Mom made it anyway.

She fluffed my hair and hugged me close. "Where's your smile today?" She took away my oatmeal and sent me off to play.

I peeked into the playroom at my sister serving tea.
Her dolls and bears were all invited; everyone but me.

The grouchies sizzled. Then, I snapped!
She had my bear named Ted! The grouchies'
words came back to me and this is what they said.

"Grouch and grump at everyone you meet
throughout the day. Don't be nice to anyone
and you will get your way!"

I snorted a disgusted sound and jumped up on a chair.
I grabbed for Ted and yelled at her.
I pulled her dolly's hair.

Much to my amazement, she looked real hurt
inside. She ran to go tell Mom and cried and cried
and cried. Mom was disappointed. I saw it in her
face. She moved me to a quiet room.
I slowly took my place.

Later at the playground, my friends played in the sand.
Joe and Hanna waved to me. I didn't lift my hand.

I kicked some sand and grumped at them,
creating such a scene. They left to play
with other friends and said that I was mean.

Dad said it was time to go.
He was upset with me.
The grouchies jumped and sang their
song with grumpy, gloomy glee.

"Grouch and grump at everyone you meet
throughout the day. Don't be nice to
anyone and you will get your way!"

Back at home, I stomped upstairs to play all by myself. The grouchies stomped along with me. They climbed up on my shelf.

I spread my brand new pirate puzzle all over the table. I tried to make the pieces fit, but I was just unable.

This annoyed me. I was mad. I sent the pieces flying.
My room became one big mess. I really felt like crying.

After dinner, Dad asked me to be his super pal. He
would wash the dishes if I dried them with the towel.
I really didn't want to! I said I wouldn't try! The
grouchies made me jump and yell with their nasty cry.

"Grouch and grump at everyone you meet
throughout the day. Don't be nice to
anyone and you will get your way!"

I was finished. I gave up.
The day was just so bad.
The grouchies' scheme did not
work out, all were sad or mad.

Bedtime came. I wasn't happy. My parents tucked me in.
Dad held me close. Mom kissed my cheek and lifted up my chin.
She asked me why I was so grumpy all throughout the day.
I told them how the grouchies came and said I'd get my way.

Now my friends won't play with me. Mom and Dad weren't glad. My little sister cried all day. And I feel really bad. Mom whispered softly in my ear that things would be okay. Dad said we all get grumpy, if the grouchies get their way.

Dad said the grouchies could be strong and make their way sound good. But rude and grumpy actions are never understood. Mom said she heard the grouchies' chant when she was five like me. She found some ways to lock them up and toss away the key.

Dad told me that happy thoughts
could shield me from attacks.

Mom said choosing to be nice stops grouchies in their tracks.

Running off some steam, Dad said, puts grouchies in a trance.
Draw a picture, sing a song. Don't give them a chance.

Mom's gentle hug erased my fears. Dad's words were always true. If they could beat the grouchies, I knew that I could too. Tomorrow I will be a friend, much nicer than today. I'll smile. I'll share. I won't be mean to try to get my way.

I hugged my teddy bear and closed my sleepy eyes. I filled my mind with happy thoughts instead of groans and sighs.

Morning came. The grouchies tried to push me out of bed.
I held them off with my new plan, and this is what I said.

"Smile and speak to everyone with kindness in your voice.
Grouchies go away, I say! I've made smiles my choice!"

Note to Parents

by Mary Lamia, PhD

Everyone feels grouchy sometimes. That feeling you get when you notice every little problem—no matter how tiny it is, no matter how good the rest of your day has been—and it makes you crabby. A grouchy mood can negatively affect how you think or feel about anyone or anything.

HOW GROUCHINESS FEELS

Underneath "the grouchies," a child may be feeling tired, hungry, bored, helpless, anxious, stressed, ashamed, or guilty. If he hits his brother and then feels bad about it, he can become grouchy and not know why. Or if her first soccer game is tomorrow and she's nervous, she might become cranky. When your child is grouchy, he may be unable to understand his feelings, or he may be having difficulty coping with what he thinks or feels, and this may result in a negative mood. A child who has "the grouchies" also often ends up feeling lonely and misunderstood.

SOME WAYS TO BEAT THE GROUCHIES

It's important that you maintain a neutral or positive outlook without shaming your child for her negativity. Drawing attention to your child as a grouchy person may send a signal that you think your child is inadequate or problematic and that it is he (not his actions) that is negative or unlikable. Shaming will not only make him feel worse about himself but will also do little to help him feel less cranky. It may even discourage him from expressing his feelings, especially those uncomfortable or "bad" feelings like anger or frustration. Instead, helping him personify his mood as "the grouchies" creates an atmosphere where your child may eventually feel safe to share his feelings or accept your help that will aid him in managing his mood.

You may never be able to determine exactly why your child is grouchy, but you can be certain that when she has "the grouchies" she does need your help. Here are some things for caregivers to think about or do to help a child who has a negative mood.

• Acknowledge the negativity of your grouchy child by offering to listen or help. You might say, "I know you're not feeling too happy right now, and I'm sorry about that. What's going on? What can I do to help?" Ask your child what she thinks may have created her grouchy mood. Invite her to discuss her feelings with you at the moment or later. You could say, "I've noticed that you've been a little grumpy today. Is something upsetting you? Why don't we talk about it and try to figure out why the grouchies got a hold of you today?"

• Help your child learn to express her negative feelings in safe and appropriate ways. You can do this by modeling positive behaviors and reactions when you're feeling grumpy. For example, if you're having a bad day, you could tell your child, "I'm not feeling too happy today. I guess I'm a little grumpy. Want to take Daisy for a walk? I think that will help me feel a little better. Fresh air always makes me feel good and a wiggly, smiling dog even better!" You can also talk to him about what to do when he feels grumpy before the grouchies temporarily take over, which they inevitably will at some point. You can use books (like this one) as a jumping-off point for a discussion.

• Make certain that your child is getting adequate and restful sleep appropriate for his age. If a child is tired, grouchiness can result. Generally, children ages 4 to 8 need around ten hours of sleep a night. If your child isn't getting enough sleep or seems to be having problems sleeping, consider talking to his pediatrician or do a little research to find tips and strategies for setting up useful bedtime routines and getting your child to bed earlier.

• Help your child to be aware of how her behavior affects others. If she has imposed her mood on a sibling or friend, help her to recognize how this behavior has affected the other person. For instance, you might say, "I know you were frustrated because you and your brother couldn't put the puzzle together right away and so you threw the pieces on the floor. Do you think your brother felt frustrated too when you threw the puzzle pieces on the floor?" Or "I'm sorry playing with Keisha and Paolo wasn't as fun as you had hoped because you didn't get to do everything that you wanted. And I know you didn't mean to get angry. Do you think they felt upset when you got mad?" Although she may deny that she is concerned about it at the time, looking at her behavior from the perspective of how it makes another person feel can help over time. And it is likely to increase future possibilities of her thinking before acting.

• Redirect your grouchy child by suggesting alternative behaviors, such as drawing, listening to music, reading a funny book, or playing. The caregivers in *The Grouchies* offered tricks to help their child that included running off steam, engaging in creative activities, and making a conscious choice to be nice. These are options any child can use at the current grumpy moment or in the future. Talk to your child about what makes him feel better when he's feeling grumpy and come up with a list of things he (and you) can do to get through the grouchies.

• Help your grouchy child learn to accept, or think positively about, situations in his life that may be unpleasant, uncomfortable, or a perceived hindrance to what he desires. You can use this as an opportunity to talk about how grouchiness isn't always the best response to these situations. You can also model a positive outlook for him when obstacles are presented in your own life. This may provide a valuable lesson for your child in coping with life stressors.

• Guiding children to seek comfort and connection when "the grouchies" are present can protect them from the isolation that may result from a negative mood. Talk to your children about who they can talk to when they're feeling a little grumpy—it could be you, a teacher, an older sibling, or another trusted adult. Let them know that sometimes just "talking out the grouchies" can be a big help in feeling better.

With patience and understanding, you can help your children understand and get through their grouchy moods and back to being their happy selves. A child who is perpetually in a negative mood may be exhibiting signs of anxiety, depression, or stress. If this is the case, seek consultation and evaluation from a licensed psychologist or psychotherapist.

Mary Lamia, PhD, *is a clinical psychologist and psychoanalyst who works with adults, adolescents, and preteens in her private practice in Marin County, California. She is a professor at the Wright Institute in Berkeley, California. For nearly a decade she hosted a weekly call-in talk show,* KidTalk with Dr. Mary, *on Radio Disney stations.*

About the Author

Debbie Wagenbach, better known as "Miss Debbie" to the children who come to hear her storytimes at Burlington, Iowa Public Library, has been promoting library programs for twenty years. Nothing gives her greater pleasure than watching her youngest patrons blossom into thriving adolescents and well adjusted adults. She loves hanging out with her family on Friday nights. Debbie adores her 29 "niblings" (nieces and nephews) and three "great-niblings." She is warmed by their smiles and challenged by their "grouchies."

About the Illustrator

Steve Mack grew up a prairie boy on Canada's Great Plains and has drawn for as long as he can remember. His first lessons in art were taught to him by watching his grandfather do paint-by-numbers at the summer cottage. He has worked for greeting card companies and has illustrated several books. Steve lives peacefully on a lake in Saskatchewan with his wife and two small children. He still loves to illustrate but now thinks fishing holds a close second place.

About Magination Press

Magination Press publishes self-help books for kids and the adults in their lives. We are an imprint of the American Psychological Association, the largest scientific and professional organization representing psychologists in the United States and the largest association of psychologists worldwide.